Linda Rogers

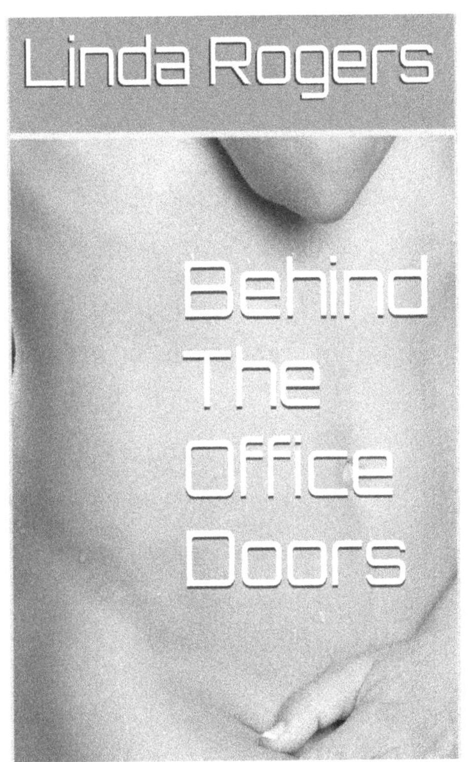

This Book Is
Dedicated To
Derek How you moved
my world and changed
my life.

linda rogers

Behind the office doors

Contents

Behind The
Office doors

Book One :

Dave's journey

Chapter

1

Life in the apartment

In a small patch of land of the world ,
in the middle of nowhere was a power
plant a dump. The power plant had
been built years before and had
contributed a lot of co2 into the
atmosphere. Next to the dump was a
massive apartment block. In the
apartment block was a small
apartment with many rooms and it
was in one of those rooms that
someone lived.

The room had a nasty smell. The
single pain window was caked in dirt
that would not come out no matter
how much it was washed. Cum lay on

the bedsheets and the window was
the only thing that provided light. The
bed was so thin that it appeared to be
just a white sheet on a plastic board.
The sleeping woman's legs were three
centimetres away from the door and
the door had woodworm. The man in
the bed woke from his three hour
slumber

Dave looked out of the widow of his
bedroom and sighed. The Light
streaming through the window was
the thing that told him that it was
6:20. It was time to get up for work. So
a depressed Dave got out of fria and
then got out of bed. He pulled on his
clothing and walked down the short
corridor which contained four doors
ando the kitchen/dining room that he
shared with his fellow . "O there you
are dave" called out sara the other
tenant. "hi sara". Dave took some
bread out of the pacet. Unfortunately
because he had bought it on sale due
to it being close to the best before

date it was all mouldy. He cut off the mould and left the remaining half in the toaster that had one of its slots broken. Jake had saved the toaster when on a night out a group of teenagers had thrown it at him while he was working. In the ten minutes that the old toaster needed to toast anything he went to wake up tod and ann. Once they were all squished into the kitchen they began to eat with their elbows hitting into people and appliances.

Twenty years ago an apartment block was built for a new industry's workers. However many years ago the apartments began to be sold off to increase the profits of the business. Some of the workers were still living in these apartments but many of the apartments were rented by people who could not afford the rent of the town. This of course caused rents to increase.

The apartment that Dave lived in was designed to hold two people however when the apartment was sold to a woman named Grace apple for 120 thousand. the price to rent went up to 1500 a week. This was money most people could not afford to pay and Dave who had been somewhat able to afford the rents before the apartment was resold was now at risk of homeless. So dividers were placed devinding both rooms and now the house had four bedrooms but very little space.In fact most of the rooms had a wall, then a bed next to the wall and then beside the bed ,there would be, another wall.

Jake and tira were a cople who shared one of the beds who got up early and had not been seen since december 25th when the household were woken from there seep by the sexual intacorse of jake and tira. Both of them had been crying out and groaning.

Tod was the guy who paid the rent. He
made sure that all of the eight people
who lived in the house payed for their
place with 160 quid and that Greg
who lived underneath the kitchen
table paid the rest.
Dave was glad that Fria, who shared a
single bed with him got up at eight
o'clock because the kitchen could not
take anymore people without the
people spilling into the corridor.

Chapter

2

When Dave finished his meal he made his way to the second door into the kitchen. This door leads outside into the corridor.

As Dave stepped out of the small apartment building he was hit in the face with the fumes from the dump and power station. He also felt the bitter cold from the outside air. He walked for an hour to the nearest train station Dave took the old train into the city. Dave knew that he was lucky that the train still went far enough to the train station he went to. In fact the only reason that the train

still served his area was because the
owner of a few of the apartments
knew that it increased the value of his
assets by at least fifty rand per an
apartment, and as he owned more
than twenty apartments he was not
going to flush money down the toilet.
So Dave got on the train so that he
could get to the job that he hated so
much but without 160 quid a month
he knew he would be out on the
street. So each day he went to his job
and tried to sell things to people. He
estimated he had made around
1,000,000 for the company but with
the company paying him 10.50 an
hour had only given him 69,000. Dave
remembered another employee by
the name of rhia.

* * * * *

Rhia had even been told by the
manager of the building "Your worth

ten million quid" she had thanked
him for his complaint, if it could be
considered one. But then the
manager had asked "o no problem I'm
a nice guy that way with you poor
people, anyway you wanna 69". She
had tried to decline his offer but the
manager then grabbed her arms and
pushed her onto his desk. His hands
had forced her clothing off and he
had taken his pants off. he then began
to push himself forwards and
backwards into her. He grabbed her
breasts and began to squeeze them.
for a full twenty minutes as the
experience was going on she
screamed in the sound proof room.
This only made the manager laugh in
fact she was only able to get free
when a phone call came in. His dick
had been on top of her but when the
phone call came in he fell backwards
and went pale. She had rushed away
and had had to leave her trousers
behind in the employers grasp. Some
of the other managers from other

buildings had come and they whistled
at her as she ran away naked.
However when Rhia had reported the
manager to the company HR
department she was given the sack
for efficacy three weeks later and
then four weeks after that the fully
edited version of the CCTV footage of
the thirty minute experience was
released online. As for the manager ,
he was given a pay rise a week after
the report to The HR department was
made for faceing "such a tough
working environment"

* * * *

It was this place that Dave worked at.
The doors to the train half opened
and he pushed them apart and got off
the train and walked the half-hour to
his office. The Sleek lift at the front
was for higher employees and
customers but for low employees like
Dave they had to climb the cheap
wooden stairs up to the 50th floor. His

cubicle door slid open after Dave slid
his keycard into the slot . He sat down
at his cheap desk that he had had to
buy and opened his computer. It took
ten minutes to start up and only was
he able to check in. The screen stated
check in at 9:00.34.88.97.34.89.29.
Dam he said remembering one year
back.

Chapter

3

Getting to work

For Dave life was filled with work. He worked one job six days a week and another for four days a week. This meant he often did not get to bed till one o'clock and at that point he would have sex till he dropped off usual at around two. So Dave was not awake one Sunday. A Sunday that would change his life forever.

It was a very stormy Sunday and the train to the suburbs was cancelled. For the workers at the dump and the fossil fuel plant this was only a minor inconvenience. For while it was a pain

to have to restructure there method
of getting to work, they knew in
advance that the train was cancelled.
So they were able to get to and from
work with a bus that one of their co
workers buddy had but for Dave it was
a disaster. Unlike the workers who
needed to get to the dump and fossil
fuel plant, Nobody had told Dave
about the cancellation so he learnt of
it halfway to the train station. A man
had walked passed and told him
about the cancellation and Dave later
was thankful that even that message
was given to him. The problem Dave
had was that nobody Dave knew had a
car, there was no bus and now the
train was cancelled. So he had to pay
400 quid to get a taxi to work where
he was going to be paid less than 95.
In fact the only reason he was not
going to just call up and say he could
not make it was that he knew if he did
that he would get fired. He began to
get wored when The taxi was a full 20
minutes late because the taxi driver

"could not find your location" Then
the road that would have taken just
one hour got closed due to a colitan
between a truck carrying a
submarine and a van carrying
kidnapped children.

* * * *

The van drivers were arrested on a
charge of smuggling, Kidnapping ,
Overriding border control , attment to
hijack a government vehicle , attment
to hide evidence of a crime and
driving with knowledge of an illegal
item. Unfortunately for them their
trile happened at the same time as a
massive crime ring was being
arrested and three were given
stronger sentences then they would
have. In fact they were given ten years
each. This was later extended to
fifteen years after the two tried to
beat a fellow inmate up and then
extended to twenty three years after

trying to escape and taking an officer
hostage. One of the pair had tried to
shoot the officer when the prison
tazed his colleague but the bullet did
not succeed in killing the officer. The
two later tried to give evidence
against one of there buyers and apon
finding this out the buyer sent people
to kill them. So the two men were
found with there head's ripped away
from there bodies in there cells. A
prison officer noticed that their
tongues were missing from their
severed heads.

* * * *

The angry taxi driver also had to stop
for diesel after the unplanned
increase in the length of the journey,
unfortunately in order to fill up they
had to go off course. The driver
cursed the leader of the country for

higher prices and Dave tentatively
suggested that possibly if the country
had embraced renewable resources
fifty years before. When he pointed
out the country was under a different
leader. The sintets had first warned of
the likes of diesel.then the driver
would not have this problem. The
driver shook his head curced and
started the car. Dave shrugged and
thought "some people just do not
listen".
 In total the fuel stop cost them
another 15 minutes..

Chapter

4

Talking with the boss

By the time Dave was dropped off at his work, it was 8:57 so he tried sprinting up the stairs but by the tenth floor he had a stitch then when he finally got to work he saw the dreaded words 9:01. He knew at that moment there was going to be trouble.

****

The company that Dave worked for was a very rich one. It provided many

goods and many services to billions of
people. As a result it owned many
large skyscrapers across the world.
The biggest one had over one
hundred floors. However this was not
to make up for a small amount of
space on a floor as on one single floor
worked hundreds of people. Each one
was given their brakes at different
times between eleven and three.
What this ment of course was that a
worker could only make friends with
two people. One that had their brake
before them and one that had their
brake after them. With two lunch
areas on each floor they fit almost
five hundred people per a floor. The
benefits of all of this was that they
could tell an employee to go to
another employee and as long as they
were not going to a different country
it would take them less then ten
minutes and as such could get
employees to use their brake for their
quote on quote "volunteer meetings".

* * * *

Less than two minutes after getting to work. Dave was walking up to floor eighty and then after that heart pumping experience he also walked the 100 metres to Tom Hardwood's office. Tom had sat there giving him a look that made Dave wonder if anyone would know if Tom killed him. However Tom did not kill Dave and instead started yelling at him for half an hour. It went on and on saying nothing of substance or advice. Simply tenths and remarks on Dave intelligence amongst other things, before he got to the point. "So first if this happens again you will be fired" dave knew it was best not to speak as it would only annoy tom further then he already was so he nodded. "Next thing is this, we can't pay you for your first hour due to you being so lazy and

disrespectful that you could not bother to be here on time". Dave had nodded and said "a yes I understand" Tom had begun his tirade of abuse once again, even going so far as to punch Dave in the nose, giving him a nosebleed and complaining when Dave's blood got on the soft carpeted floor. Dave had begged forgiveness but tom had said that he should have thought about the consequences before being late. He also said that now Dave would have to pay for the floor to be recarpeted and would also not be getting the three hours pay from 9:00 to 11:00. At the end of the day he got 42 quid for the day's work and lost 400 from the taxi 10 for his pre paid
train ticket 5 quid for lunch that he lost due to him being relocated from being on the 32nd floor to being on the 50th floor and 2000 for replacing the carpet. In total his intake for going to work that day was minus 2373. As Dave said "today was most certainly

not a good haul". In fact it was for this debt that Dave started to sell his belongings online and also went into business with fria by starting to sell the videos of him and fria having sex.

Chapter

5

Going to the manager

Dave worked in a tiny cubicle that was half the size of his bedroom. In the cubicle was a small display monitor and a small computer. He was also given a keyboard and mouse, but besides the door there was nothing else in the cubicle.

Food and drink was only allowed in the brake area. Dave had heard that when someone had mentioned this to the manager he had said "no actually the supervisors are allowed food and drinks in their workspace, and in fact have access to a nice staff room with a chef". The manager also said that employees could meet each other as employees higher up the ladder were allowed to call for the lower employees as long as they were not already in conference with a higher employee.

Dave cursed as Jake kimmel walked into his cubicle with a smile on his face. "O looks like somebody is in big trouble" Dave nodded, while he wanted to tell jake, a supervisor he really really hated, to "fuck off" he knew that that would result in the loss of his position and with it his pay. Instead he tried to be respectful and said "o could you posible explain what you mean by that " Jake came over to him. The long fingers on his left hand digging into his neck. "Well guess what ugly" said Jake cackling in glee. Dave shrugged "no I don't know what you would be here for". Jake skouled and squeezed Dave's neck "go on and guess' ' Dave gulped as much as he could with Jake's fingers on his throat " I guess maybe you're here to tell me that my brake time has changed". Jake smiled "no, that is not what I am here for". He punched dave in the stomach and began "I just got a message saying your late and well i also had a look at your history and it seems as if your on the hock for some firing" Jake had drawn a Little Rock from his pocket and had it him on the side of his head with each word he said. Dave grew panicket "Jake look it's just a mistake". Dave knew there was no way that Jake would do anything but said it anyway. Jake pushed him to the ground and stood on his shoulder "o it's just a mistake is it, is that what it is,you should have told me it was just a mistake, well with four mistakes you should know by now". Once jake let him get up he was pushed out the door. "Your going to my office you ugly little slime". Called out jake.

Dave followed Jake up the stairs to floor seventy six. Jake's office interior had been designed by him. In one corner was a small wrestling ring where he liked to hit employees. And on one wall was a massive tv that played a variety of violent shows and movies. On the walls were a small collection of guns. And the desk was so high that when Jake sat down in his also long legged chair, his feet barely touched the ground. In comparison all the other chairs had such short legs that when Dave was in Jake's office and he sat down he had to bend his legs so they touched his neck . However when he did sit down Jake's voice grew angry "ugly did you just fucking sit down without asking me" "o am ya soory a bout that i was" "you ugly were being stupid that's what you were you as usal were being the thick little pice of ugly sh" Then the phone rang it's shrill rininging would have caused jake to ordinarly tell the caller to call somebody else but this caller was the manager for the intire building. Jake listened as the manager gave him orders. Jake put down the phone and looked up at jake with a smile on his face "wow ugly aren't you lucky imign all the other employees who have never met the manager but you, you get to met them and all alone so nobody can cooperate any stories of being beaten almost to death".

Chapter

6

Rhia and Dave's meeting
With the manager

Dave grounded internally rhia had
told him of the violence that the
manager had inflicted on her before
getting fired. He did not want to
experience the violence she had had
to experience.

Dave rembered what she had told him
that once she was shown into the
managers office she said "look i just
need you to come up here at five each

day and have sexual intacorce with me and then we need not inflict any punishments" she had glansed at the man standing in the corner who dave would later know as jake, for support. The manager had seen this and said "o ya and he will watch" She had refused so Jake called in the CEO's son. "This is Tim, He's a boxer" "Ya my dad got me a fight in the boxing olympics' ' Tim then proceeded to break every rule in boxing and beat rhia in every way possible. For while he was a shit boxer, he was not. Then the manager had come over and slid his hands up her top "o you're not wearing a bra" he had cried out in enjoyment. Rhia broke down in tears as he ripped her clothing off and started to fuck. The two men had stood here shouting "fuck her fuck her" Unfortunately rhia had had her phone taken off her and the pictures of her injeres deleted.

****

In comparison to Rhia's meeting with
the manager Dave was about to have
a little less traumatic experience, but
a traumatic experience all the same.

The door to the manager's office
opened and Dave walked in. Jake left
with a smile on his face. Dave wanted
for a minute and then somebody
came out.

The person that stood there was a
completely nacked woman. Who had
stepped out of the managers in the
work bedroom. Dave Was startled
"um is the manager buyisy". The
woman smiled "o no sexsy i'm the
manager".

Dave thought about asking her to
cover herself as he could feel
something but thought better of it. He
knew you never asked the people

employing you to do something they did not want to. So instead he asked a less personal question "what happened to the other guy" "o he disappeared police say he was probably guilty of fraud but look at you" Dave nodded he could definitely feel something changing "Am i being fired" The manager's seemed to become less cheerful "ok i'll explain" "thank you that would be nice". The manager sat down in a strange chair "So you have four strikes the first for using the elevator" Dave put his hand up "what is it sexy" Dave swolad "it's just that i did not actually know about that rule" "o well sexey that does not change the fact that you did break the rule aneway the second rule you broke by sleeping in your cubicle after hours" The manager smiled and winked "i have to say watching that one helped me to reach to peak, Anyway the next two were for being late"Dave tried a fake smile "well maybe i could have another chance"

The manager pouted "i'm afraid it's
company policy so i'm going to have
to remove you" Dave's fake smile
dropped and was replaced with a sad
face. The manager got out of her
weird chair and went over to Dave.
She wrapped her arms around him "O
looks like you're pleased to see me my
little friend" She whispered into
Dave's ear as she slid her hand
through the gap between his torso
and pants. "Nice and full length". Dave
frose as his dick was moved up and
down in the manager's hands. "Am
what" cried Dave.

Chapter

7

A choice and
new experience

Dave felt the hand squeezing his dick and could not move. He had expected an assault but not this type of assault.. so instead he focused on the room. The walls are decorated with paintings of naked bodies of men and women. In one of them a man had his pants down and Dave realised that the man was fucking a cow. The man had been trying to get the cow to fuck him for years. The man's expression

of true pleasure was in contrast to the
unrecognisable face of the cow. Dave
did not know that these were not
paintings from the painter's
imagination and instead were of real
moments. So Dave looked On a
different wall were two sets of
handcuffs and The desk with it's thick
legs and chair made his dick grow
harder.The managers hand caressed
the top of his dick before she
withdrew and she said "O sorry, i
should have offered you a chair to get
cofterbull in". Dave moved to sit in one
of the high back leather chairs but the
manager called out "oh no that's for
clients you are not a client" Dave grew
confused "Well then what chair do i
use" The smile on the managers face
was wide as she said "My chair my
little sexey beast".

Dave walked behind the desk and sat
himself down in the manager's
strange chair and then felt her hands
pull off his pants completely . She

noticed his look at the unusual and strange design of the chair "So a little fact is that this chair, my sex mechene, is built for two people" the manager finished speaking and winked. Dave sat there with his dick standing up, hard at a rock. The manager sat herself the wrong way round into the chair and as she slid herself onto dave. Dave froze as his dick entered the manager and she put her hands through his soft hair. "Now my dear dave you have a chose hear" whispered the manager "you can fuck me whenever i call for you or you can decide not to do that and get fired and louse your accommodation, if you chose not to have sex with me and as a result not be my little bitch boy then you can exspect to live on the streets and die of starvation" Dave swolod hard he could feel the inside of the manager as he said "I think i'll chose option no 1" The manager pulled off dave and came right back for more "Which option" dave sighed "the option were i have sex with you whenever you call for me" The manager nodded "I think we best move into the other room" Dave Watched as the manager opened the door to a bedroom. "This is a nice little place where I keep my super king sized bed".

Dave was thrown on top of the soft bed. He took a breath in and the manager moved on top of him. Her hands on his body "ok my little sexey beast, let's move" The manager groaned as Dave slid his dick inside "O that's nice is it not" Dave felt the warm flesh press against his body as it slid smoothly forwards and backwards. He could not help himself when he said "o ya that's good". The manager looked at him and called out"you liked that, then try this" Something changed suddenly he was on top and her hands were on his large breasts. He felt her hands squeezing his breasts and pulling him closer and

then once he was fully inside he
pushed back "Ya that's" his voice was
cut short when she pulled his head
forward and began to push her
tongue into his mouth. She turned his
body over and over again. Each time
she did Dave pushed out and in again
and that would cause the sounds to
rise in desirable levels.

Chapter

8

The bedroom

The manager's hair tickled Dave's face as she kissed him again and Dave kissed her back and began to grone himself. The managers hands moved off of daves breasts for a moment to place his hands on her breasts "if you want to push off from something then push off this" she whispered. Dave smiled and said "thank you i will" then he felt her warm soft hands slid down his arm and begin to play with his ass by squising it It was half an hour later that the manager said "o ya ya, hey do you want to stop this" Dave knew it would be a bad to tell the truth and say "no i don't want to stop doing this, I want to keep fucking you forever" So he said "i guess" "well then lets change things up a bit" Dave found his face on the pillio as the manager bent down. She placed her hands on daves ass and shok it "o ya just like jelly only tastier" then she began to lick the outside of his butt "o thats strange" said dave "it's good though" dave smiled "o ya come on do it again please" "ok shue will" The managers tongue slipped into the crack and soon her lips pressed onto dave's asshole and she began to stick her tongue into dave's ass "i like this" "i do too". The tongue that licked the inside of daves ass along with the tingling sensation of her long brown hair on his ass and the messaging of his breasts gave him a strange feeling. Dave was groaning when The manager cried out in ecstasy "O ya this is good" Then she thought for a moment "but i don't wanna keep it all for myself" Dave smiled and the manager said "hey how about your turn" dave got up and turned the manager so her face was to the pillio and coerced her breasts as he lowered his tongue to stick in the managers ass. Daves young son touched a solid object in her ass and swallowed it. He whispered in her ear "Do you keep food in your ass cuz if not i just ate some of your shit" The manager smiled and said "o ya well there more where that came from " Dave looked at her "a deliver on the way" "o ya it's coming just like me". When Dave's tongue got around the piece of shit he could feel the muscles in her ass push it onto his tongue. He pulled out and kissed the manager on the lips and let the shit pass between them. The saliva from both their mouths mixed with the shit and the resulting mixture was pushed back and he swolde it. The manager cried out "can i have some of you waste"

Dave nodded " shure ". Dave placed
his dick in the manager's mouth and
hot urine began to squirt out like a
fire hose. The manager drank and
drank and then said "well that's one
dick juice gone can i have some of the
other juice" " o ya you can have that
all day long" Dave cried out. The
manager began to suck daves dick
and he could feel the tongue on his
skin and that brought the juices
coming.

When they were both tired they
slotted Dave into the manager and
slept as one. Dave had his dick inside
the manager and she had her arms
around him and two hours later it was
five o'clock. "o is that the time? " said
the completely nakaed manager.
"Well I guess it's time to go home."
Dave was sad. "Do I have to?" The
manager got up and moved to her
tallboy. She picked up a plastic card
and and walked back over to dave
"See this" She asked "Ya, what is is"

Asked dave "It's a nice key card for the lift" "o are you saying" "yes each morning you take the lift up here and we fuck" "Ok that sounds like a nice time" The manager pushed dave into her and said "i'm shure it will be" Dave groned in plesure and said "It will be the best exsperence of my life".

Chapter

9

Off home

The manager gave Dave his trousers back before pushing him against the wall and kissing him. Then she squeezed his breasts and gave him back the rest of his uniform.
He was in a daze as he walked out of her bedroom and into the office. He opened the door to the elevator. Dave took his key card into the lift and marvelled at the lift's beauty. There was an expensive piece of artwork from a renowned artist that probably cost a few hundred thousand. Each button had gold around it. Then he

noticed the buttons. There was
something strange about them it was
only when he was walking down the
marble entrance that he realised that
there were no buttons for floors 10 to
64. In other words you could not use
the elevator for getting to the ground
workers. Dave walked the twenty
minutes that were needed to get to
his second job. The fancy restaurant
needed "people to entertain" the
customers. So each day dave and his
partner sara hops would "entertain
them" Dave and sara were the music
group. There were other groups
available that did other things. One
group performed magic for rich
children, another danced and
another one full on stripped. The one
thing in common with all the
entertainers was that they provided a
sexual service. The rich and powerful
liked to feel as if they could make
people perform tasks that they would
otherwise not have performed,

simply due to the power that the rich and powerful hold.

The restaurant had decided not to let its main employees such as its waters to suffer this and stopped it from happening by giving those who tried it on waters, food poisoning. One very rich and elderly man had taken his hand down a female waitress and squeezed her but. He died three weeks later.

So the restaurant employed the likes of Dave to get the sexual assault.They would darken the room and give the customers control over the lights in there cubicle and then if the guests wished they could turn out the lights or leave them on, but when they were ready the guests would fuck the entertainment.

Dave went up the side entrance and got into his easily unzippable costume. He did not like his job too much and it had been only thanks to his low sperm count that he had not

fathered around twenty children. For
each day he fucked over six women.
He opened the door and went along
the third floor. The restaurant was
divided into three parts. The ground
floor was for the fancy eaters but bills
generally did not cross the four
hundred mark. Then on the second
floor were the millionaires and the
billionaires. The second floor was
open plan and had a lot of expensive
artwork and the floor had cost over
thirty million quid to build. Then on
the third floor we're many pods that
separated groups of guests. There
was a swimming pool in the centre
and it was on this floor that Dave was
on. He walked over to the sixth pod
and pressed the entertainment
button. The occupant turned out the
lights and Dave went in.

He felt the hands in the dark run up
his naked leg. They pulled him
forwards and off his feet. In an instant
he was swept off his feet and was

entering the manager. Dave Did Not
No That The person in the pod was
the manager. He had thought
something did feal similar about the
way that they were fucking him but as
he was not the best at catogrising the
customers he fucked he did not know
who it was.

Dave finished at ten when the
restaurant was only open for private
bookings and Dave had not been
blocked.
 He walked for half an hour and got
his train home. After walking through
the door he headed into the kitchen
and made his dinner. Unfortunately
he had to wait half an hour for one of
his house buddys to finish making his
meal. Dave sat down and ate up his
food and satisfied the hunger "Note
to self, Shit , piss and dick juice do not
satisfy your hunger" he said.
After his dinner he headed up to the
bedroom. He pulled off his work
clothes that he had changed into to

avoid the drunk rapists on the street.
Then fria called out "harry has his
family over still" Dave sighed. He felt
so tired but knew the only way both of
them were getting to sleep was if the
were inside each other so he
composed himself and said "ok so
how do you want to fuck me".

Chapter

10

Going to work

Dave was inside fria until 12 when he and fria fell asleep. The next day Dave rose bright and early he made his way downstairs and made some breakfast. Unforcenitly tira knocked over his breakfast unto ground. "Dam" he said "i'll have to make some more". So Dave once again made his breakfast and after consuming it left the apartment to go to the train station. On his way there he met someone from apartment 249 "o hi are you going to work to" The man

from apartment 249 shook his head
"no no i'm heading off abroad" "o
going somewhere nice" "Well france"
"o that's nice" "Ya" The nabor licked
his lips nervously "well i'll go now" "by
then".
Dave walked to the train station and
got on the train. The smell of urine
was rank and did not make Dave's
dick stand straight as the manager's
urine had done when it was in his
mouth. Dave sat down in the
unoccupied seat and tried to avoid
getting his legs in the vomit. When
the train stopped he stepped out and
tripped on a pothole grazing his knee
and falling into a puddle. Dave cursed
and walked the long walk to the
office.

Chapter

11

Manager privilege

This time instead of going round the back and climbing the 49 flights of stairs he walked through the marble and gold lobby and passed the women and men in suits and to the elevator. Once in the elevator he pressed the button to the manager's floor and the elevator rose like a bullet. He marvelled at the amount of money spent on just this elevator, Money that would take him a good few lifetimes to captain. He stopped pondering when the elevator doors

opened and he was met with a door
that stated "Managers office" .He
tried to open the door but it would not
open so He pressed his card against
the reader and the door clicked open.
He walked into a hallway one led to
her office, one led to her bedroom
and one led to the living room. He
walked through the door to the
bedroom and saw the manager with
her back turned. She was naked from
the torso up. Dave came behind her
and ran his hands down her legs as he
pulled off her trousers and
underclothing. "o ya i like that dave"
"there's more where that came from"
dave slid his hands up her legs until
they were messaging her ass and
then he moved them so they were
massaging her breasts. She cried out
in ecstasy "o now that's very good".
She stood there for five minutes and
then she glanced at Dave "o look at
that you're dirty" dave squeezed her
breasts and said "o yes i am very
dirty". She said "you want to have a

nice bath" "if you want it". The two of
them ran up the stars in the room up
to the bath that was more like a pool.
She jumped into the pool and said
"dave strip off those clothes" Dave
obliged and jumped into the large
bath he grabbed the manager and
said "o ya i like water" she smiled and
pulled him inside her. "come on push
your way inside" "no problem". Dave
noticed a float in the water and
nodded to it and said "you wanna do
some oral" "why not". She climbed
onto the float and Dave said "no let's
put one hole to another" so he pushed
his mouth to her and began to stick
his tongue in. The manager grabbed
his head and forced it against her
hole. Dave's dick was standing
straight and the manager began to
rub her hand up and down his dick.

Chapter

12

Lunch time

As the building began to replace have of it's staff work time with a ten minute lunch time that some had thought of reporting to police for braking employee treatment laws. The manager and Dave were isolated from all the work of the day. All that exercise while not burning much calories had made both of them very tired and hungry. Dave said "would you like a pizza" " well If i can eat it off your chest then why not" replied the manager. Dave nodded and called the pizzeria ``am so my address is" The

manager slid off the float and slid her
mouth down to his dick and began to
suck it. Dave was saying "and finally a
15 inch peperone" The manager stop't
sucking at his dick and said "and I
think I'll have a 15 cm hot dog" as she
caressed his dick. Dave hung up the
call and looked at her "I can do about
that." He sat down and once again
began to stick his tongue inside her
hole as she began to wrap her lips
around his dick. They lay there for
sometime taking pleasure from each
other. When the pizza finally arrived
dave was resting on a float in the pool
the manager went up to get it. She
came to the door naked and opened it
to see a delivery driver standing
there. She took the pizza and placed it
in the lobby then she pulled the
delivery man into the room and
kissed him. "I just need you to come
with me". The delivery driver followed
her into her bedroom and said "what
do you want". She grinded "just you"
she lay on the bed and moshend for

the driver to sit down "i'm danny by the way". "Ok danny how do you like this" She split her fingers into danny's pants and began to give him a hand job. "O let me make it easier for you" said Danny as he let his trousers fall to the floor.She Pushed him onto the bed and began to push her way on top of his dick. "I can give you ten minutes". The driver placed his hands on her nakid breasts and said "o ten minutes would be perfect".

Chapter

13

An erotic delivery

After she got the driver to return to
the door she pushed him angst the
wall and toungn kissed him said
"goodby my little sex delevery" and
then shut the door in his face as he
said "i was wondering if i could have
your number" . She returned to the
pool with the pizza and Dave said "o
pizza" and opened the box. "It's a bit
on the cold side is it not said dave
The manager pertended to sigh "I
know these people can't be trusted

can they" "ya" "I heard that a bunch of them have sex while on the job" Dave laughed "o on the way" the manager nodded "shure, on the way, not because the people they dilever to presure them into it".Dave looked at her at took a slice of pizza as he ran his hand through her hair and along her face. He took a bite of pizza and then after his fingers left her mouth he kissed her. The pizza passed into her mouth and then back again. This continued and as it was happening he got his hands on her breasts and coresed them his hands continued to move down her torso and down her left leg then he moved his hand back up her leg and then to her vagina. Then he pushed his fingers inside And took another bite of pizza. "i 'm gonna have a slice of that pizza now"

Chapter

14

The letter

That night as dave and fria were fucking each other to get to sleep a speshel deliver was pushed through the small appartments letter gap. The Next Day tira came to the door and picked up ten letters. Tina was very surprised,She had never seen there be ten letters at one delivery. "Maybe they found a bunch of letters from way back" she pondered.But if that was the case, then why did all of the letters look the same. She put them in nine different piles, Two for Tom and

one each for everybody else. She picked up her one and then without opening it left for work.
Around an hour later Dave came down and noticed his letter. "o look i have a letter" one of his other flatmates said "yes we all do" "and there all without a postage stamp". His flatmate decided to lie to Dave and said "O ya i noticed that". Dave said "well anyway i need to get to work so" he picked up the letter and walked out the door. While he was licking the manager's vagina she said "you seem like you received some news, o ya i like it that way". Dave took his tongue out and wiped his lips. "well i did receive an unexpected letter". "So you haven't read it yet" Dave shook his head "ya i'm going to read it on the way home".

* * * * * *

However when dave was on the train home that night he had forgoton the letter and insted was thinking all about ways he could fuck the manager. "We have done oral both ways and at the same time and did it in the pool, I wonder if we could do it in space". He entered his apartment complex and wondered why it felt so irrey then he noticed the lack of lights. Why were all the lights off then as he walked down the stairs to his basement apartment he saw a group of people in hard hat's and one woman without one.She seemed oddly familiar "of dave hi". The manager looked at him and smiled.

Chapter

15

The work meeting outside of

work

Dave felt he needed to get some answers so he asked "Am Can I ask what's going on". The manager nodded "well I own the building". Dave was in shock"what did you say". "Well when I saw your sexy little cock after your pants were strped off by that fella ryan, I decided to buy your apartment". Dave nodded "so your grace apple" Grace bowed "yes i am indeed grace apple" After two seconds grace said "i know your probably in awe that you were inside grace apple but it's ok". "So you

bought my apartment but" "well as i
said in the letter i have decided to buy
the whole building and convert it".
Dave nodded "that must have cost a
lot". Grace shook her head "No no only
around one hundred and eighty
million". "O right one hundred and
eighty million" "i mean currently while
it does sit around five thousand people
it is not a lot of space for them" "ok so
you want to expand the space but have
less people" "exactly, i mean how about
ten flats per room then have two
bedrooms a living room a dining room
and a kitchen and two bathrooms, or
in other words seven rooms , seventy
flats and just under four per a floor" "
So you want to go from having around
one thousand five hundred flats to
twenty four" "yes about that yes" "you
do know we need more homes not
less" "well currently i can make around
one hundred million from this place,
but if i was to go ahead and just
convert it then that number would go
to around two hundred and fifty
million". Dave looked at her "your
going to charge like eleven million

quid for this location". Grace smiled "o sorry i didn't tell you that i also bought the energy plant and the dump" "ok, am so how much did this cost you all together". Grace pulled up her phone and looked at the calculator app. "O around seven billion". "O right that's a lot" grace nodded "yes it is". Dave looked at her and said "but wait where will i sleep". She looked at him"inside me of course".

Chapter

16

A new place to fuck

She opened a door to an apartment and stiped off. Dave followed her into the apartment and got his hands on her side.her hands pulled of his trousers .He looked her in the eyes as she lifted him up into the air.Her body slammed against the wall as she forced him into her.Her hands ripped off his shirt in the dark and she began to caress his breasts.She pushed forward through the open door to the bedroom and onto the double bed. He shouted out" o ya let's do this". For five minutes she moved forwards and backwards,up and down. Then suddenly the door opened and in the darkness a man went to his bathroom and brushed his teeth. He slid himself into bed and then Grace pushed herself on him. The man let out a little cry as his dick began to harden. Grace then pushed herself onto him and turned her back to Dave. Dave pushed his dick into her but and the thresom commenced.

Chapter

17

The journey in style

The stretch limo pulled up and grace pushed Dave into it. She got in and watched as Dave marvelled at the inside of the limo.He looked at the massive flat screen tv, the game's consoles, the drinks machine and the small pool and toilet. There was also a small bed. "You rented all this' ' he said as he raised his arms. Grace's face changed as she shouted "oh hell no" "so we're not supposed to be in this limo" asked Dave in puzzlement. Grace shook her head "no I own the limo". Dave nodded "very cool". He pressed the button on the drinks machine and a bottle filled with orange cola.dave took a sip as Grace moved to look up at his head. "Hey have you ever fucked a woman in a car" .Dave choked on the drink "am well no actually, I never had enough to get a car". Grace smilled "would you like to try something a little bit new". Dave grinned "shure why not". The driver turned down the volume as the groans and cries rang out. Then the driver put there foot on the pedal forcing the car up to 120.

The stretch limousine stopped outside a small mansion. Grace said "here we are ''. Dave got out and looked around "you have a nice home". Grace nodded "o ya it's ok, I mean it's not as good as the main one but". "I'm sure we can manage '' said Dave as kissed her on her lips. Dave felt her hands slip into his underwear and start to fondle his dick.

When he broke away she licked her
lips and said "aneway come with me".
Dave follows grace through the house
and onto the small port. Grace turned
to him and said " ok my fuck
mechene, tell me witch do you want".
Dave was confused "witch what, do I
want ". Grace said " we'll want a boat
that will take us to our destination of
choice in under a day or do you want
to take the over a week long
experience in the super yacht". Dave
did not spend even a second to think.
He simply said " I think that I will take
the super yacht".

Chapter

18

Sailing home

The two of them went onto the boat
and as Grace plopped herself down in
a massage chair Dave marvelled at
the leather walls. He looked around
the boat, at the bedroom that he
would sleep in , the bar where over
one hundred different drinks were
stored,at the onboard pool that was
bigger than an olympic pool. He also
saw the massive toilet that held the
thickest, softest and best smelling
toilet paper. As for the toilet, Dave
thought it looked more high tech then

his old phone from two thousand and
fifteen. He washed his hands and
drred them. He did not realise that
the total that he used was made of the
rarest cotton in the world. Dave
walked across the bathroom and over
to the shower. He stripped off and
grace who saw him and smiled and
joined him. She whispered in his ear "
you know this glass is supposed to be
shatterproof, well I was wondering if
you might go ahead and help me test
that " . Dave backed into the glass wall
and moaned as he came in and out of
grace. He looked at her and pushed
further in we're he stopped and
stayed for awhile. She kissed him and
squeezed his breasts. Their warm
fleshy texture was so good in her
hands. The two of them crossed each
other's breasts ``o ya I like this' '.

****

They slipped into bed and Dave lay flat on his back as Grace stood with her legs bent to get Dave into her. The feeling of ecstasy was Divine. It continued for the week they were on board.

When they arrived grace said "unfortunately we thought due to riseing sea levels it would be stupid to build a house next to the water" Dave nodded "ya smart, you don't want your home flooded and you being unable to sell due to the ever aproching sea putting off any potential buyers". Grace smiled wryly "ya but what it means is that we have another ten minute drive ahead of us". Dave shrugged his shoulders "I'm sure it will fly" grace winked "I'm sure it will"..

Chapter

19

A new home

Dave got out of the limo and pulled on
his trousers. He looked at the gates
behind him as they closed.The gates
were fifty foot high and so were the
walls. The house in front of him was
massive. Dave said "it's like five times
as big as my entire apartment block".
Grace got out of the limo and told the
driver something. The limo left and
the gate opened for just the right
amount of time to let him get out.
Grace joined him and noticed his
stare. "o ya the house, i know it's a

little small for your main house but we like it". Dave asked a question "how many floors are there in the building". Grace said "well there are four main floors and then there's the lower attic where we keep the servants, the upper attic where we have things we don't need but want to keep and finally the top attic for all the insulation. O and the basement for storage ```"well at least the basement is ordinary ```"yes i know we had to install a lift to get down to them" Dave was confused "A lift ```"yes i mean for six of the basements they would be a lot to walk". Dave watched as grace showed him inside. "do you want a tour". Dave laughed " well of course i want a tour". "ok so let's start from the bottom up" "just like you did last night" "o ya so i did". Dave followed grace into a lift. Dave marvelled at the size of the lift "it's bigger than my apartment" "i know,but the best part is this speed dial here" "o what does that do" "well you can choose from the lift taking one hour to go from the top to the bottom to the lift taking just 20 seconds" "that's cool" "o but how about you sit on the couch and i climb on top for 20 minutes" "shure why not" "oppa here will video us" "thanks oppa". Dave got on the couch and pulled his lower clothing off and gasped as Grace's body came on top of him. The lift slowly went down and down until the ding filled the air and the voice said "basement six".

Chapter

20

A strange tour

Dave walked out into a massive area with cages. At first he thought the cages contained dogs but then he looked again and saw that the cages atual contained humans. "whats this" "well one of my little side buisness is pornogapy" Dave could not beleve it "what did you say" "look seven months ago i read that your place has the highest rate of workers haveing sex at work" "what the hell, is that true" "yes it is , aneyway i had to get a job there to get some of that sweet fotage" "o relly" "yes i know and i got it and i was very happy to discover ten years worth of pornogerpy reddy to realece". Dave could not believe what he was hearing "and you released it" "well yes, i did and it was very good,very well received on my websites". Dave moved his head from side to side."did ya make much". Dave saw Grace take out her phone "well from that we made about ten million"Dave chucaled "wow that's a lot of dough" "I guess you're right, from one little mine I guess it is, I never thought of it in that way ". Grace thought for a second "but we got like 50 million from the folk here" "how many people do you have here". Grace pondered for a second " i'm not sure how many but the basement extends 1 kilometre on either side and about 100 m in width" "anyway this is a bit boring so let's go up". Dave followed her back into the lift and for the next five minutes as she sucked his dick he lay in an erect daze. He was woken from his trance when the lift opened on a floor that was filled with white

powder. "Wow, that 's cocaine" Said
Dave in a joking manner. Grace
however did not pick up on the joking
tone so responded by saying "how
The hell did you know" Laughed
grace. Dave was confused "is n't it
dangerous having cocaine in your
basement" "well the main entrance is
about two kilometres away" Dave
nodded "but what if Grace laughed so
well then we do this" She went back
into the lift and pressed a button. A
thundering roar began and to protect
himself Dave covered his ears "Grace
what the hell is that" "well my sexy
little bitch that is that" she shouted
over the sound as she pointed to a
section of the wall. The section of the
wall that was about a metre thick
began to move across until it fully cut
off the right section of the tunnel.
"wow, that is" said david in a shocked
voice "i know pretty impressive". Dave
shook his head "how much do you
have" "o around two billion quid
worth""ok two billion, right". Grace

nodded "ya I mean we have to have multiple distribution points elsewhere for effeminacy". Dave said "so how much over all". Grace chewed her lip "well I would say around ten billion". "O that's impressive" said Dave.

Chapter

21

The food of madness

Dave And Grace Returned to the elevator. Dave was in shock. He had expected the usual rich person wastefulness such as multiple pool tables, a personal movie theatre and the like. He did not exspect a pornogorfy empire grouped with a coke empire. He should have begun to feel fear as he was trapped under four floors of rock and dirt. If She wanted to leave Dave down with the cocaine then she could. Nobody would ever find him here. She could say that he had been fired and everyone would just assume that he had become depressed and killed himself. But this did not go through his head instead he had his dick erect and grace was softly feeling it. "nice and hard". The Door opened to a room filled with harnesses and people. "o let's ignore that particular floor ok" said grace with apprehension "ok" said dave. They got into the elevator and it rose to basement three. The door slid open and the stench of raw meat hit him. "O it's a kitchen" Dave guessed. Grace shook her head "no it's not a kitchen" Dave frowned "so what's with the raw meat". "Well around ten years ago we were dumping like '', She counted on her fingers ``like five hundred people a week, so we thought why not diversify and remove waste problems by selling human meat". "You sell meat '' Grace nodded "ya I mean you would be shocked at just how many people want some nice human burgers ``''cannibals' 'Grace shook her head. "No no, not just cannibals''. Dave scoffed "who else exactly would buy human meat". "Well there are people who want to play pranks, you know the whole "you just ate a human and did not notice a thing", actual" She said "we have seen a bunch of YouTube and other online social media pranksters buy at least a million quid in meat, it's kind of disgusting to be honest". "So it's a leucritive business then" grace nodded. "Do you want some" Dave shook his head "I'm fine thanks" "shure but if you change your mind just ask" "thanks" " i mean all the slaves are feed it and they don't complain, I mean, they did at first, but then we just turned the ones who did into food for the others, so". Dave smiled "how nice, am I don't mean to rush your grace but could we possibly

get back into the nice stench free
elevator " Grace nodded "ok, I guess
they do say if you see how meat is
produced you will not want to eat.
Anyway on words with the tour".

Chapter

22

A strange collection

The elevator came to basement two. Dave was almost sweating with apprehension. What would be inside basement two. Would there be a sweatshop with lines of children being given Barely enough to eat or maybe if possible something worse. The doors slid open and inside was a massive corridor lined with art.Dave sighed in relief "it's art" Grace nodded "I mean we have around one hundred pieces of art upstares ". Dave nodded "o right you don't have space". Grace shook her head "well no that's not it we could put a least fifty more upstairs " "ok well then what is it" "well the artwork down here is sort of stolen so if it was on display it would be returned to the original owners".Grace paused for half a second before saying "you know governments always saying "o you can't just buy things that were stolen from an ancient sacred temple" ,we have tried to pay them off but they still wouldn't remove the laws" she stopped speaking and composed herself. "Anyway we have a few of the works of hitler that were stolen from a congressman in Texas and well there are so many to count". "O, right" said dave in a horse tone.

Chapter

23

The Basement

So to go over, in bacement six there were pornslaves, in basement five there was cocaine being dealt , in basement four there were people hung up on harness in basement three there was a meat plant for humans , in basement two there was thousands of stolen artwork and now they were going to be entering basement one what would be here. What horrors await dave. The doors opened and revealed rows and rows of vehicles. There was a mix of bikes, Cars, Trucks, Vans , boats and

even a few small plains. He also noticed
around ten different style helicopters.
Grace pointed to a massive steel part of
the wall "that lets us drive up a ramp
and into the outside world". Dave
walked over to a helicopter and said
"could we posible take it out for a spin".
Grace pondered the thought for a
second before saying "ok i don't see why
not". The trailer that the helicopter was
on connected to a DNCC 23. Grace got
into the car and started the engine and
Dave slid his way into the passenger
seat. The car moved forward as Grace
pressed a button to open the hatch.
The two of them got out of the car and
got into the helicopter. Grace flew the
helicopter high above her home. Dave
marvelled at the world below and said
"look everything is so small". Grace
winked "I know a few things that look
small but are actually fairly big". Dave
looked behind the house and saw a
large stretch of tarmac. He thought for a
second before saying "am grace" grace
turned to face him "ya" "what's the long

stretch of tarmac" he responded. Grace nodded " o ya that's our private runway". "Your what "well when we have to go somewhere and we want to get there fast, we fly ". Dave nodded "so you have your own private runway" "ya took us so much bribes to get the planning"."o cool".

Chapter 23

A Helicopter Ride

The helicopter landed on a small helipad on the top floor. Of the apple mansion. Grace hopped out and after looking to see if she was ok and it was actually safe to jump so did dave.She walked over to a small keypad and pressed nine buttons then she placed her finger on the keypad scanner. There were a loud two clicks in quick succession and Grace got a magnit she had taken from the helicopter and pulled A door open, Grace walked through the door and moshned for Dave to follow her. He did as he was moshand to do and came down the large flight of stairs to the 4th floor. There Grace showed him her massive kitchen. Instead of ordinary chairs there were ten thrones the thrones were placed along a massive table. "This looks like it came out of a palace" said dave, "well it did" confessed grace. Dave looked at the coffee machines and kettles and toasters, all things you might find In a random household. However these appliances were buffed up. Then you had the not so ordinary appliances that Dave could not even recognise. Dave and grace moved into a bathroom the size of an average house. A cold pool lay on the left and a pool filled with hot water lay on the right. Grace explained that both had a wave mechan. At the back of the room were four doors. One at the far left lead to a steam room another on the far right lead to a Sana. The one the left just before the end wall lead to a full gym and the other on the right hand side lead to grace's bedroom. Or as grace exspaned "the place were you will be fucked by me every single day".Dave and grace spent some time in the pool together. Dave liked being inside grace while being in the water. After an hour Dave explained that he was very tired and attempted to get Grace to call him to her bed.When Grace took the hint she showed him to a chamber that would suck all the water away. Then the two of them journeyed into grace's bedroom. They were both completely naked.

Chapter

24

The Bedroom

The bedroom was large. The whole room was the size of an apartment costing a million quid. In a far corner of the room was a bed with ten different sex toys on it. The sex toys were covered in a slimey substance and the bed was very inviting for Dave. beside the bed lay a contraption that had many pulleys and straps. On the side of the contraption we're printed the words :
The dene roboticsany fuck mechene mark three
Grace looked at it and smiled "hey my sexy little Dave" Dave said in an

uncomfortable tone of voice "a yes" grace said "could you get in the harness" Dave did not want to get into the harness but he also did not want to make grace angry. So he slipped on the straps and sat himself into the harness. "So what'a this for" grace looked baffled "well it's for fucking of course". She got her body on top of his and began to push him in and out of her. Dave whilst having a fully erect dick, was feeling somewhat uncomfortable."o could we possibly move to the bed" asked Dave. Grace shook her head her hair swinging from left to right and back "o no we are going to stay right here". Grace picked up a key button next to the harness and pressed the button that showed two people in the middle of sexual intacorce. The Locks click it shut and grace hangs the key button up on a key rack. Dave did not particularly like this new situation.The contraption stopped him from getting up and continuing the tour. He asked Grace if he could "Continue the tour now if possible".

Grace shook her head and said "o no there will be no more walking about" Dave looked at grace. She smiled at him and said " now your going to stay right here and be my little toy". Dave was in disbelief , He could not comprehend his situation. why had grace done this. For what reason could she have had to trick him.As if she could read his mind she said "well it's like this, my little toy , i need to have my little bit of pleasure" .

Chapter

25

Tim's day

Tim was in shock. When he had gone to check in for his flight to France he had discovered his passport was out of date and he would need to renew it. So he returned and ignored the workmen. He had gotten into bed and then suddenly felt a hand go over his mouth as his dick was shoved up against something. Then once it had become hard the person had gotten on top of him and before he knew what was happening he was being fucked. He had not enjoyed the experience until there was a great shift and another dick began to shove it's way into his bottom.this had been the first time in two month he had had sexual intacorce since he had broken up with his boyfriend five months before. The two of them had tried to rekindle there relationship by having sex in a tolit at a restaurant but were unable to do so. This had been some of the best sexual intacorce in years and something inside him was hungry for more. He stood still as his passport photographer took the picture. They nodded "there you are sir". They handed him the photographs and he stared down at them.``thank you" he said automatically. He did not even know that he had said it. Tim walked out of the shop and to his home. He began packing his things away. A workman took down his bedroom wall and another scooped up the pieces of wall and the pieces of urn that his great grandfather had been preserved in. Tim watched as the remains were added to the massive pile of rubble out side.he took out his phone and called his office.

He was feeling strange and this feeling
was making him act in a strange
manner. As if possessed by an evil spirit
that wished him harm he talked with
his supervisor and resigned from his
post for health reasons. This surprised
the supervisor but he did not say so.
Tim stopped speaking but did not hang
up. For ten seconds he stared at the red
round circle and wondered why it was
red and not blue or some other colour.
He was pondering this question when
the supervisor grew annoyed at waiting
for Time to respond. The supervisor
clicked the button to end the call and
then pressed the intercom to say that
"Terry got back to work".

Chapter 26

Grace Has Her fun

Dave was sad that night as grace forced herself into him. She told him that now he could never leave. "I gave you a nice bit of time off to go on holiday". Dave said in a subdued tone that he would love to go to Greece. Grace laughed and said ok his fake body would be found in Greece in a month. He said "what, you're going to kill me". Grace shook her head and said "no I'm going to fuck you"

One day, Dave had lost track of the days, Grace was squeezing his breasts and licking him all over when a man came in. Grace had Dave inside her and her tongue was inside Dave's mouth. The man came up behind grace and pulled her back into him and off Dave.

Dave cried out "leave her alone ''. Grace shook her head and said "no no Dave he is not going to do that, are you" she looked at the man. Dave also looked at the man and said "well if you know him, as you seem to, then who is he ''. Grace smiled and returned her gaze to dave. "Well my dear Dave, this man right here happens to be my husband".

Chapter

27

____

The Husband

The husband looked at him. "So I see you have another one". Grace nodded "this one is almost grade A tier". The husband smiled "are you sure you're not overreacting". Grace shook her head "no no I'd say after six months we should move him to the basement". Her husband smiled and slipped his hands onto her breasts. He closed his eyes and groaned. He pulled her into him and kissed her lips. When he pulled away he said "well if he is going to be placed in the basement he needs to be tested. Grace and her husband stripped off.her husband pushed her onto the bed and pushed himself inside. He grabbed her breasts and kissed her.. it continued for twenty minutes before the husband came off her and towards him. Dave saw the husband urinate all over him. When Dave cried out the husband caused the urine to enter his mouth.the husband looked at him and said "some people enjoy" he paused "abusive stuff, so". The husband left the room and returned with a horse whip. "Had to go all the way to the stables to get this" he said as he wiped Dave on his face, his torso and his back and then he hit his dick Again and again.

Chapter

28

A nice little party with all the mates

The people arrived through the basement. One of them was a king who had sold many people to the apple's. Grace smiled as he entered "Jim, welcome to our house".

****

Jim was a very deep mystery. He appeared to be in his 20s or 30s but that had been the case for many years. In fact when he first arrived in the country

he was to become king if he was a man
in his fifties or sixties. He had wowed
the queen of the country and had then
married her. Later she misteryl died
and he became the ruler of his own
little country. He had soon after began
to publicly force his people to do slave
labour. He had for years had slaves but
had kept it secret. After a few years he
began to send his dead the apple's in
exchange for money. Then he became
the head of the drugs imported into his
country. One person had said to him
"why is the king taking money for being
in charge of illegal drug distribution".
The man who had asked this question
found himself, a very short time after in
an apple minser.all in all Jim was a
strange man who was a king but still
kept slaves ran a cult and was involved
in illegal activities all the time.

****

Jim also brought a massive box with him that he had left for the contince to be minced. "I was playing a game a while back where I locked everyone who came into one of my homes and it was so much fun I thought I'd try it again" Grace smiled "yes as you should". Jim continued "well when I did a ton of people did not play along so I had to kill them" "o that's good, we did need some more meat" remarked mr apple. Jim clicked his fingers "o and could I get some for my rabbits" mr apple nodded "shure don't see why not".

Another guest came in "o sorry to hear about losing the head of the police force race harper '' said Mr Apple In a tone that he tried to sound sympathetic even though at heart he did not care. Harper responded in a slightly angry tone "well I would have won with your help". Mr Apple nodded "yes, yes you would so I guess next time don't stop an investigation into that man who owned that shop". Harper sighed "o ya I forgot about that, I'm sorry , I'm sure it will not happen again '' Mr Apple nodded "I'm sure it wouldn't happen again as well".

The next guest was a wealthy billionaire. He was racist anti-unionist and a man who wanted to use earth as a testing ground for devices that might assist him on another planet where he would live only with people who would work for him. He was also a person who instead of being referred to as "man" he hated to be named as he was opposed to public relations. He had bought millions of followers online and was always pandering to them. One day he decided to try to buy access to ban those who said bad things about him. Then one day a jornalust told him of a story about to drop that he had sexual propersiond one of his female employees. He then claimed that soon attacks would increase on him. He breathed a sigh of relief as his followers labelled the article as false. But for now he got his sexual expotation from mr apple's bacement.

The final guest was a very powerful man who had connections with many fascist party's across the world. He had placed over ten dictators in power. The man had a very large hand in Mr Apple's business. He had helped Mr Apple reach the connections that he had needed. The man went by the name of harry. However Mr Apple knew that he also used the name James among many others.

The billionaire and Harry recognised each other "o Derek, I see you here" said the billionaire.. Harry had helped the billionaire turn his fathers millions into billions. One of the companies the billionaires had invested in had a major competitor from china. Harry had perverted the competition from expanding.

Chapter

29

Dinner is served

The party interred the party dining room. Next to it was a large kitchen where ten chefs made fine meals for the guests. The wine came out and was powered by water and water. The billionaire took a large gulp of wine and grabbed the leg of the water then offered to buy the waitress a car if she felt his dick. Mr apple put his gun to the side of the billionaire's head and said "hey, ok harry is not going to be helping you out of this one if you don't start

understanding one thing" the
billionaire skoyled "o and what's that"
mr apple smiled and put the gun back
in his holster "well you pay me for the
sex not them". The billionaire was about
to respond when his glass was filled
with wine. He drank from it and began
to change. The wine bottle had an
alcohol content of sixty percent. Mr.
Apple cackles with laughter "a little
concoction from my vinarad in
thessaloniki, alcohol is added to make it
nice and alcoholic".the billionaire
smiled "your one piece of shit aren't
you".

The group after their starter meal that
cost more the ten thousand per a
person continued and as the people at
the party began to drink more and
more they became more an more open.
Mr apple said "you know I got a ton
more money than they think". The
billionaire nodded and laughed "ya, you
know a while back I bought like a couple
of million on a cryptocurrency" Jim

nodded "ya and" the billionaire licked his lips and said "well then I told a ton of my followers online that I had bought some" jim smiled "o I can see where this is going" the billionaire nodded "so these idiots assumed that it was a good idea to buy into it" jim said "and then" the billionaire laughed "then I sold my cripto for a couple of billion" harry said "it was lucky you weren't arrested for miliplating the market" he paused to take a gulp of wine "I mean you should have been". Mr Apple said "well good thing you're a billionaire anyway".

After a main meal that cost over one hundred thousand the group moved on to the desert. Grace announced at the start of the desserts. She held up her hands "look I know what it looks like but these muffins are made of the rarest chocolate and flower" she paused." They also have a good serving of cocaine in them, in fact it's best not to eat more than four or you'll overdose".

The billionaire grabbed three and
began to eat.

The group continued to eat and drink
far into the night. More and more food
came out and ten bottles of wine were
drunk. A further fifteen bottles of beer
and two bottles of gin, brandy and
whisky in fact the only thing that
stopped the group from getting alcohol
poisoning was the puke drink that
made them vomit up their food and
drinks like a rich Roman.
Once the food was all gone save for a
few buns that the apples did not want to
risk killing one of their guests with.
They went down to have sex with some
of the slaves and after the night's
entertainment went back to their cufer
driven cars. The billionaire got back on
his private jet and returned home. The
apples retired to bed and fucked until
the morning.

Mr apple left on a business trip in the
morning and grace gave his dick a

squeeze before saying "get someone to do this for ya will you, I don't want you to go without out sex for half a month". Mr apple nodded "don't you worry I'll have it seen to".

Chapter

30

The morning after

The sun was shining through the four pane glass of the apple's kitchen window. Grace came out of her room after fucking Dave for an hour and a half. She was tired as she had had no sleep with all the fucking. Grace Looked for a nice tasty snack in the snack cupbord. The visitors had cleared most of it out and the servant in charge of replacing the food had been killed after it was discovered that she had been disapproved of the treatment her and her fellow servants had to insure each day. She looked distally at the crisps which were a flavour that grace hated and then saw some muffins. "Ok they'll do, '' she said. Grace Got a beer from her massive fridge. She Pulled the throne forward and sat down. She felt very hungry and bit into one of the muffins. The cholite chips tasted so good she wolfed down three more muffins and drank half of her beer to wash it down. Her mind began to become clouded and she grabbed the remaining muffins and ate them. She began to go to the window to vomit. However as she bent over the balcony to vomit into the pool below she bent around the balcony to try and get it in the water. There was a bit of urine from the previous night of passion with her husband and as she pulled her head to be underneath the balcony her head went dizzy at the same time as she slept on the urine and fell four stories to the poolside concrete floor with a hard thump. Her face smashed into the concrete and blood spilt from her wounds.Then her torso and legs swashed into the edge of the pool forcing her body into the water.

Her face scraped along the side of the pool as it slid into the water. Her face was broken in multiple places.

* * * *

Grace lay there in the outside swimming pool for half a month until her husband came and dumped her body in the pile. However three nights later one of her husbands security met with a friend who worked as security in daves office. He told him how "miss apple had not gone to work in seventeen days" the drunk sequirity to graces husband said "ya i'm pretty shure that miss apple is gona be turned into mince meat by her husband" "what i gota tell the police" "i'll i can say is that the fucking phico is probably gona kill me next". The security officers drank well into the night. While graces husbands security officer forgot his story the other security officer did not

forget and in fact got a friend of his to
do some digging

Book two:

An

investigation

Chapter

1

Mr apple back to businesses

Mr Apple looked down at the pool were his wife had died. He unlike her was on the 1st floor. He pondered the pool and then got on top of the balcony. He jumped and plunged deep into the pool. He was lucky that his pool was twice as deep as an average pool because had it been an ordinary pool his legs would be broken. Mr Apple got out of the pool and skowled "the stupit bitch could not manage it, That was easy". He walked over to the outhouse where a woman wanted him. "O you're all wet" Mr Apple smiled and said "well I'm definitely wet now". The woman stiped off his cloths and he pulled of her's. He pushed her body in to the outhouse wall and pushed his dick into her.

Mr Apple and the woman moved out of the outhouse and pulled on new clothing. "I'll take you back to the sex club while i'm on my way. The woman smiled "that would be very nice of you" "i know it's nice, It's very nice". He got into his BMW and pushed the button to open the gate. He roared past the gate and drove away

Chapter

2

It's A world of many different jobs

In this world there are many many different jobs: many of them, such as the job of an author, are possibly simply because people are willing to pay. Their jobs are either not necessary or made necessary by people and their society. Fred Hops was a private investigator, a job that many might want with the exception of dirty police officers.. Fred was fairly good at his job, and had on multiple occasions broken the law to assist in an investigation. Now He watched as the gate opened and was

going to sneak in but a bmw He looked
at the high walls to mr apple's house
and then went to his truck. He got out
his 30 foot ladder and placed it on the
wall "i can jump from that" he said. He
climbed to the top of the ladder
attached a bit of string to the ladder and
jumped as high as he could. His fingers
grabbed the top of the wall and he
slowly pulled himself forward . Lucy the
wall was more than a metre thick and
the spikes did not bother him while he
had his special clothing on. He pulled
the ladder up and then slid it 50 metres
to the ground. He braised himself and
jumped. His face smashed against the
wall and his legs shook when they
contacted the ladder. He climbed down
and landed on the property. He noticed
the security lasers and stepped over
them he pulled out his gun and shot the
electrical wire. The power went out as
Fred opened the door and stood by the
security system. He spread a spray on
the keypad to stop it from
communicating and pressed the keys

that the security officer had told him. The Alarm changed from on-faulty to off-working just as the generator kicked into power."That was far too close for my liking," said Fred.

Chapter

3

Investigation into a basement

He walked over to the elevator shaft and forced the massive doors open with his knife. Then he looked up and saw the elevator. He clipped some of his 50ft rope to the bottom of it, grabbed the elevator wires and began to drop down. However soon he was out of rope. So he braced himself and untied himself from the pulley system. Next he slowly dropped down to the bottom and was very thankful that he had the goodsense to wear gloves. He pried the door open with his knife and saw the rows of people in cages. He stepped closer to one cage and saw two people in the process of fucking each other. He then noticed the camera recording the event, a massive mountain of white powder he walked over and put a few spoonfuls into a plastic bag. Then he returned to the elevator shaft and was about to start climbing up one of the wires that the elevator ran on. When he noticed a hatch on the ground he tried to open it but it was tightly shut. "Ok well I'm going to have to get that open, " he said. Fread began to slowly free climb one of the wires and was way up the forth basement level when he lost his footing and fell. Luckily he caught one of the other wires and stopped himself from falling to his death. He knew that if the fall did not kill him the elevator would finish the job. So he climbed up to the fourth basement level and opened the door.

The room was filled with the sounds of horny men groaning and grinding.Fred walked over to the people and pressed the record button on his hidden camera. One of the horny men said "hey mate this bitch is taken". The man then tried to scream as Fred hauled him over to the lift. Fred tried to push the man into the lift. He was planning on interrogating the man. But instead of falling to the floor of the massive lift, the man fell two story's down and cried out before his spine shattered and his neck broke. Fred cursed soundlessly and stepped back into the room. He pulled another man away and asked him what was going on. He said "my friend told me to come here" . The man said "well this is the fuck tunnel" Fred turned his head to one side "the what tunnel" the man knodded. "Well it's here that you get y to o fuck women all day long" Fred nodded "so it's a brothol" the man opened his mouth to say something before nodding his head, then the man felt he should say something so said " well I guess it is it's just that there is just so many options here". Fred nodded so your rapeing them. The man smiled "I guess we are" .

Chapter

4

The man locked up

Grace apples bedroom was a very nice room. It had nice artwork and had everything you could desire in a bedroom. However some could not feel that it was a nice room. Dave hung poised in the air in the harness. The woman who came to feed him, take his waste and also rape him cointinued to come. She was paid for every day of work she was not about to remind her employer of davees existence. However when Dave had asked her where grace had gone she had told him if he asked

her any questions that she would
remove his tongue. So Dave lay there
each day spalding out.Whenever
something would itch he would feel it
but was unable to itch.

****

One day as the food he was given were
the remains of the apples meals he felt
sick. The reason was that a week before
the apple's had taken a very rare and
large fish, the remains of which were
enormous. So for a week all that Dave
ate was this slowly rotting fish.so on the
eighth night Dave began to vomit.
However because the harness
perverted him from moving he vomited
all over himself. The next day he had
had sex forced on him by someone who
said afterwards "I mean as you know I
have fucked a lot of people" mr apple
had said "of corce my king" "but I have
to say I have never fucked somebody
coved in vomit". That night grace had

said she wanted to see just much vomit was in a person. So she had taken a feather from one of the peacocks and forced it down his throat. He had gagged but the feather continued down. His eyes began to tear up and he heard rather than saw grace laugh. "O look at him cry the little cry baby, o do you need your mama , do you want to go home, o wait I forgot you have no home" the guests had laughed and said "o my he looks so sad and pathetic". Grace then took out her phone "o by the way we were having a little bonfire and we needed some fuel" she began. "So we decided to use your belongings" she stopped and added "o and some of your friends". She should him a photo of his roommates and rhia on spiks surrounded by his belongings. He could also see grace mid laugh with a flamethrower in her hands. The flamethrower had flames burning rhia and he could tell she was screaming in agony. He tried to speak but instead vomited all over himself. The king laughed "wow you idiot you actually fell for all that". Dave sobbed "wait it wasn't real". The shook his head "it was ai, all we said was rhia surrounded by Dave's belongings being burned by laughing grace with a flamethrower.grace said "ya the photo is fake but it's a lot more tame than the actual photo". Grace smiled and Dave said "wait so it did happen" grace nodded and said "maybe it did, who knows not you at least". They laughed and left him alone.

Chapter

5

Fred's investigation
gets some more people

Fred had reached the third floor. He gagged as the stench of meat fit him like a train. There were people in gas masks making meat. There were ten mincers that meat was being thrown into and from the minser there were meatballs, burgers , sausages and more being made. He could see a crate market stake. And another marked human fillet.

He could not comprehend why exactly there was a meat processing plant in one of the basement levels. Then he noticed the sign "do not consume meat, raw meat is dangerous and even cooked human meat may cause madness". He realised now why nobody had found the body of the police officer who spent ten years undercover and was about to reveal the identity of a massive drug dealer. He was shocked but still managed to pull himself together and pull himself up to the next level.

Fred was a man who spent a lot of his time on his job. He read up cases and spent three hours a day researching case's.he could recognise much of the artwork. One was a mosaic that was put into the floor and had been stolen from an ancient site in Greece. It had been bought by a billionaire who bet it in a poker game with mr apple.
He also recognised a painting stolen from the Guggenheim museum in America. "So my dear friend has a nice

little underground museum of stolen
artwork, that is interesting".

Fred rechid the next floor and saw
many expensive cars and other
vehicles. He then got back up to the
ground floor and took out his phone. He
pressed a few buttons and the screen
was lit up with the number of a very
senior police officer that Fred had
helped. The police officer had one of the
people involved in a case get away on
their yacht. So Fred had told him not to
worry about the injustice and had
snuck on board. Fred had placed and
explosion device on the yacht and when
they were out in the middle of the sea
he detonated the explosive device. The
explosion killed the man and the police
officer thanked Fred and told him if he
ever needed him just to call. So when
the senior police officer picked up the
phone Fred said "am I a little criminal
for you" he paused and then continued
"o and this guy is powerful so best to
keep it off the record for as long as you

can" Fred gave him the address and hung up.

The police arrived and broke down the sequirety to the house of mr apple. They made there way into the home and searched through the basement Levels. It was just as the private investigator had said "drugs,prisoners and stolen art and a lot of meat". They took pictures and samples and one officer got a bag full of cocaine on the sly. It was a few officers that had sex with some of the prisoners. One of them identified the body of grace. Now that they had their reason to enter justified they needed more people to take care of the sprawling mansion.

Chapter

6

Lockdown

They police called in backup to lockdown
the house. They began spewing into the
house. Some went up stairs, some went
down stairs to the basements and some
stayed on the ground floor. It was ten
minutes later that they Discovered Dave
in the harness. They helped him get out
of the harness and brought him to a
transport vehicle.Then some of the
officers brought him back to the station.
Other officers began to load the prisoners
onto trucks that had arrived. In total
12,346 people were freed from the
basement. And 300 body's were

uncovered. It went from concern from a sequrity officer to a murder incuire by a private investagator and finaly to one of the biggest raids in the history of the country. With A Valuation of over 100 billion the house of mr and miss apple was a significant enough dent in local crime. Furthermore the sudden surprise of fifty private investigators surrounding the properties that connected to the bacements ment that the police were able to arrest and imprison over 5000 criminals connected to the apple's.

Chapter

7

___

The Secret Room

When police were told that there was probably a secret room below the sixth basement they at first laughed. They thought that the private investigator was insane. One of the more senior officers said "wow so they built six bacements were highly illegal activity's we're going on and built an elevator to them, but when they decided to go deeper they made the entrance in the elevator, which would have by the way cost millions, wow are they stupid or what". But when the investigator kept telling them to go down there they were convinced to at least attempt it . So Officers carrying a blowtorch made their way into the

elevator shaft. The elevator had to have
been removed for safety sake. So in the
end it took two days to prise the locks to
the secret room open. They knew that
while they did not know what they would
find, if the basement kept up with its
theme of illegal activity , then there would
be something not so nice in this Heavily
protected section .The officers watched
as finally the trap door was released. It
then took a massive winch to pull the
trapdoor off. The officers could tell that
the trapdoor was Hevey . In fact After the
door was weighed it was discovered that
it weighed more than fifty tons. Officers in
gas masks walked down the flight of
stares that the trap door was blocking.
The officers walked down over one
hundred foot. On all the sides were
squares of wood. It was discovered
afterwards that this wood was one of the
most expensive woods in the world.
The officers continued to shine their
torches down the long staircase that also
had multiple very thick doors every few
feet down. In total they got through
twenty three doors. When the stars finally

ended they walked out into a large space
that one officer said "looks like a mall".

Chapter

8

Fun Times

The officers looked around the large room. It contained all the past times you might want with the exception of anything that needed to be serviced or kept up. It was for this reason that there was no pool on this level guessed one of the officers. However there was many tables with games such as chess, checkers,mankana and many more. At first they thought that would be all.they believed it to be a not so little "man cave". However then they saw the stares and walked down it. It was here that they

saw the rows and rows of cans. Tens of
thousands of large cans filled with food.
The officers could see all the different
flavours. Then at the back a massive
pool filled with all different types of fish.
Next to it lay the filtration system that
kept the water clean. Then the waste
from the fish was piped to the plants next
to it. "O, look who has a nice little
renewable food source" said one of the
officers. "But how does he power it" the
officer shrugged "let's find out". The
officers continued down to a bedroom
and relaxing floor were a massive
collection of over one thousand dvds.
"Does he still have dvds, wow I mean
streaming has been a thing for decades
now". There was a massive movie room
that contained more seats than beds in
the entire area. Further from the stars
was a gaming area. There were four
gaming monitors at both gaming setups
and each had a custom pc the size of a
car. This time when the officers looked at
the hundreds of titles they did not scoff
and instead a few of them pocketed
some of the more expensive games.

Beside the entertainment area there lay two massive beds. They were custom made to fit eight people each. Next to them were two double waterbeds. And then dotted around the place where there were a few Cochis and armchairs. "So this is the sleeping area". The floor below it came as a big surprise to the officers.

Chapter

9

Energy

On this floor was a massive machine. that on examination it was discovered to be an energy production unit. Massive vats of dead fish that had not been eaten and massive piles of fish faeces were used to make electricity. One officer had asked "an how efficient is that". He had been told they did not know yet but "he had to find some independent renewable source of electricity while he was more than two hundred foot bellow the sea level". They could see a massive battery with a reader on the side. On it were displayed the words "enough power to last an estimated : ten years " . An officer whistled "wow that's a lot of juice ". What the officers did not see was a massive machine at the very back that looked a bit like a drill. The massive machine was designed so that two, or three at a squeeze could drill their way up to the surface or if they wished further out and if they got bored of the stares, down. This floor was bare of any fake walls. It was one massive endless line of gas tanks. The officers noticed a sample of the wall and for the first time could appreciate just how thick these walls were. First there was fifty feet of limestone with an unknown substance to keep all the bits in one piece then there was a two metre thick sheet of tungsten then four metres of concrete then a metre of steel. After that was two metres of cement and then a single metre of lead and then feet of grafen. And then nine metres of corrugated iron after that would be a half a metre of whatever material they wanted the wall to appear to be made out of.``wow that is a lot of protection" said an officer looking at the chart. Another one came over and said "I wonder how much this thing cost". The first officer nodded "I mean the walls cost at least a few million". They also looked at the lines of oxygen tanks. "There must be at least a thousand of them" "I'd say around ten thousand" "but what are they for ". The officer pointed to the stars that had been revealed when they pushed the wall out of the way "let's go ahead and find out". His fellow officers nodded and they began to climb the stairs to get deeper into the bunker.

Chapter

10

Mr Apple's Meeting

Mr Apple Was in a boardroom meeting as a heavy investor in Apple who owned Five percent of the company. He was well used to the jokes about his name. "Mr apple investing in apple" but in spite of that he felt he needed to be there. So when he got a call from one of his less reputable contacts he did not pick up. Instead he thought "why is the fuckless man ringing me now, I'm in the middle of

a meeting". What this meant was that
when he left the meating to go to his
BMW instead of being prepared he was
accosted by the police. They said "mr
apple could you come with us please". Mr
Apple did not want to look bad in front of
his fellow apple investors so went with
the police men. "My wife went missing, "
he explained to his fellow investors. "O I
hope they can help you out" said one of
his fellow investors in a sympathetic tone.
What Mr Apple or the other investor did
not know was that The police were taking
him to their jail transportation. Mr Apple
thought they might want to talk about the
disappearance of his wife. He did not
worry about this however as he had a
story made up to explain it.

****

One of the officers was glad that mr
apple had come without a fuss. He was
used to rich people being very annoying
and Unfortunately the other police officer

by the name of bill that excorting mr
apple was a dirty cop and had actually
spent a large chunk of his money paying
for mr apple's sexual slave service. He
had also worked with Apple's empire to
protect them and even to create dirt on
police investigating Mr Apple's business.
What this meant was that as his college
was closing the door to the jail
transportation van bill pulled out his gun
and placed his finger on the trigger. Took
off the safety. He aimed at his colleagues
head and then fired point blank towards
bill.

****

Mr Apple on the other hand was not
pushing triggers and instead was
pressing a button on his watch that was
supposed to issue a message to tell all of
the people who needed to know to save
him. However unfortunately for Mr Apple
it had never been tested as he had not
wanted to cause confusion. This meant
that when it failed to send Mr Apple

began to get very concerned for his safety. He did have many people high up as ether friends or as people he bribed.However he worried that if he was not able to contact them in time or if they did not see the report earlier enough he would be in danger. But he did not need to worry because at that very moment somebody was trying to solve his little issue.

Chapter

11

Bill's Success

Even though bill was trying to aim to kill
and while being the kind of man who paid
people to have sex with other peopple
agenst the consent of the people he was
having sex with, he was not the best at
fireing a gun. In fact the last time he
actually hit his mark for the first time was
two years before when he shot a man
with a knife while being ten metres away.
He had celebrated this small victory by
walking towards the man who was lying
on the ground with a bullet through his
neck and began firing seven more bullets

into the man. One of them missed the
man.

****

Bill's shot had missed his calling
completely. It instead hit the truck and
went halfway through Mr. Apple's left leg.
Bill heard the cry of pain and thought he
had hit his mark. Bill's colleague acted
very quickly and pulled out his pepper
spray and spread it into Bill's eyes before
he could fire another shot. Bill dropped to
the ground, tears streaming from his
eyes. His collage wrapped her arm
around his neck. He whispered in his ear
"Look buddy, you try and shoot me i'll
make you fucking pay" Then he twisted
bill's neck and broke it.he laughed "I've
always wanted to do that" then He threw
bill's body into the back with mr apple
and got in the drivers side. He took a look
at mr apples phone and saw a message
from friend of his saying they should
listen to the blues and reds and that he
believed that he had some at his
home.The officer had no idea that this

was in fact a badly coded message and
that this was a piece of evidence pointing
to his guilt. He pressed the button to start
the vehicle and drove to the jail.

Chapter

12

The Hospital

The police hospital was a very grim
building. It had bars over every single
window and patients often had a gun
pointed at them at all times. In fact twenty
percent of people admitted to the hospital
died for so-called "security reasons' '.
The gates opened and the police truck
came in.

****

When mr apple was brought into the jail
they noticed the gunshot wound. The
officer transporting him had said "well
when I was getting the truck ready to
transport him bill was making sure that
he did not try to run away" the jail

progress reporter said "yes go on". The officer nodded "well he grabbed bill and". At this point Mr apple interrupted with the words "that's a dam lie, I am Ryan apple and you want to take this pice of felths word over mine" the jail officer looked at him "please shut the fuck up, I'm trying to do my job". He had turned to the officer "anyway please continue". The officer had began "well he grabbed bill and broke his neck and then he was running away so I tried to stop him. Then after that I shot him through the leg to stop his flight". The jail officer wisiled "wow you are very lucky that you are an officer in this country, I mean in a different country they would probably distrage you.the officer smiled "o I'm fully aware of that". The jail officer said "anyway that gunshot will have to be seen to" "what do you mean by that" "your going to have to take him to the jail hospital".
It was clear he did not want to but the officer did his job and returned Mr Apple back to the truck. Another jail officer came with him to escort him to the

hospital and to stay there until he could
be interviewed.

Chapter

13

A powerful enemy

The nurse bent over the hanged man and smiled. She was used to the brutality at the hospital. When a person had no friends or had enemies in high places they would end up here. Many politicians whose friends had deserted them after they lost power had spent time here. One poloton had blackmails his way into power but when a hacker leaked a ton of government files online one of the things that was leaked was all the info about his blackmail. One of his victims had tried to blow him up so he had landed in the deadly hospital jail. Mr Apple was not aware of halo salawanka. His friends that he bribed did not tell him they were also receiving hevey bribes from mr salawanka. He thought that it was only a number of small groups that he shared when they told Mr Salawanka of his massive trouble and the amount of evidence against him Mr Salawanka had decided to try and ruin mr apple. Mr Apple controlled around forty six percent of the world's drug trade. However Mr salawanka controlled another twenty seven percent. He knew that if he could eliminate mr apple without directly killing him then he would be able to seize mr apple's share of the market and would control seventy three percent of the market. This was such an attractive proposition that he at once had some of his friends place Mr Apple in the brutal care of Greengate hospital jail. He had made sure that mr apples case be moved to the top tree of security. What this meant was that Mr. Apple's identity became a number. It also meant that he was blocked from contacting anyone and even was gaged to prevent his identity from being leaked. So as Mr Apple lay strapped to his hospital bed his leg slowly healing his empire was growing smaller. He had made many enemies with his arrests. People felt that his bribes would stop and that Mr Salawanka's bribes would continue. It was for this reason that the thousands who had supported him were now supporting only mr salawanka.

One day Mr Apple had tried to get to a phone but had fallen to the floor and had to crawl. A nurse had asked him what he wanted and when he told her he wanted a phone she held one just out of his grasp. He had moved forward to get the phone and the nurse moved back. After ten minutes, Mr. Apple managed to grab the phone in time. However this victory would be short lived as the nurse then kicked him unconscious.

Two weeks later Mr Apple was released from the hospital. His leg would be damaged forever but for now he would be able to walk. It was advised that he use crutches but it was thought that he might try to use them to escape, and had he been given them he would have.

Chapter

14

The Interviewer

Mr apple sat in the interview room. "So mr apple we have discovered illigle narcotics in your home,multable slaves you use for the iligle sale of pornogerpy via streaming and also slaves that are used for sex both those things also come with kidnapping charges, We also discoved hundrads of stolen pices of artwork and have records of over fifty thousand murders including one of the officers who tried to escort you here so what's that about". Mr apple said "look i'm not doing or saying a thing until i get a layer". The interviewer signed "ok well when your lawyer gets some time to assist his client i shall be back to continue". The interviewer moshoned for mr apple to be brought back to his cell."I can't keep waiting for his lawyer to arrive so just take him to his cell"

****

They unlocked the door to his cell and pushed him in. The gard thought "must be a stark contrast the inside of a cell used for drug users that's filled with piss and a massive multi million quid mansion". His thoughts were interrupted by mr Apple when he said "hey am can i ask you a question" The hard pressed the record button on his voice recorder and said "What's your question prisoner Seven Four Eight Three Nine Two Three" "i was just wondering if you'd be in need of money" The gard snigered "well if you were offering i do need to get a mortgage". Mr Apple licked his lips ``how about ten million" the god shook his head "no no, i'm risking being fired for accepting a bribe so fifteen million ```"ok fifteen and you let me go ```"shure". Mr Apple sighed in relief "ok so once you let me go i can get a new identity and then i can just disappear" The guard laughed and took out the voice recorder he pressed the end recording button. He walked back to the cell and tazed mr apple through the bars. Mr apple fell to the ground with his leg twitching. He screamed and Then the jail guard said "you can fuck off mr apple".

Chapter

15

Taking The Property

The police had raided mr apples
house and the property that connected
up to his house but Then The Police
also raided severely other properties
that the apple's owned. A movie studio
was discovered to have been dealing
drugs on a massive scale to all the
people involved in films. Many fans got
angry at this because there ip could
not be used to make more movies and
now the 30th movie in a very popular
movie franchise would not be made.
Daves old apartment block was

searched top to bottom and then a thermal imaging camera picked up people moving below. When the police made their way down they discovered a methamphetamine super lab and arrested the people there. A manshon in the south of england was the home to the child sex traficing for the people of the royal family.

While many of the people who were found to be using the apple's service were able to escape from justice. An example was a duke who should have gone to prison for seven years but instead escaped and in fact it was never even filed.

Chapter 16

Dave's Statement

At the station dave made a statement on the last three months. "So at first i thought it was just an office romance but then" "then what" "well then i was shown the drugs the sex slaves and the stolen artwork". The police officer looked up "and you didn't report it" "well no" the police officer began to get angry "and why did you not report it" "well i happened to be a bit tied up". "Right, well I guess then it can be excused". Dave was silent for half a minniet as the police officer filled out some info. Then dave

asked "am can i ask what happened to grace" "grace" "grace apple". The police officer nodded "o yes, well she is persumed dead" dave said "what the fuck did you say". The police officer said "well we have a witness who says that he saw her husband dump her body into the meat processing plant"."how did she die" The police officer read off a report "well she sustained multiple injuries to her stomach,arms,legs and head"
"Am have you confirmed her body" "well" said the police officer "we tested for DNA and found yours and her husbands. "O right" "yes you had semen in her mouth and her husband's blood from his penis was on her teeth". Dave nodded and asked "could i posible see her body".

Chapter

17

The meeting of the police

officers

The car stopped and the driver handed
his ID card. The security guard checked it
and punched in the code to raise the
barrier. The car entered the car park and
found a parking spot. The car pulled to a
halt and a police officer got out of his
police vehicle.

The officer walked into the large building.
He walked down the corridor and up to
the door where an officer stood on guard.
The officer took out his ID and showed it

to the officer on guard. The officer
showed him in and he saw Greg Goodon,
head of the entire police force.
Greg looked at his files In his office. He
had recently been promoted to the job
after the previous head was suffocated in
his home. Greg was saying "So what
your telling me is that we have just
seized sixty billion worth of stolen artwork
drugs and assets bought with dirty
money" The police officer in charge of the
apple investigation nodded "ya, It
appears that the apple copple were
collectively worth around four hundrad
billion between smart investments and
just direct money from illegal activity".
"How many crimes are they gilty of
exactly " The police man in charge of the
apple investigation pondered for a
second "Well there is bribery, tax
exashon, although that might be argued
down to tax avoidance, then there is drug
production, drug sale, drug traficking ,
Sex traficking , Sale Of Pornogerpy ,
Forced sexeual intocorce , Rape , child
rape , child kidnapping , interfering in
elections of a democratic nation, Stealing

, Purchase of goods with knowledge of theft and around one hundred thousand cases of murder and a lot more" "ok so there most likely going to be gone for a good while " "ya probably, if he was ordinary, it would be life". Greg looked at the files "o I see he has a bunker what's that for exactly". The police officer said "well it looks like a shelter over two hundred feet in the ground that was designed to help those inside to survive a nuclear strike or worse" "I wonder if it's also for protection against other people in his industry" "I guess that is very possible Greg goodon said "so what kind of dent will this make on crime" "well it will probably take around two months for them to be fully replaced" Greg goodon nodded "And of course it won't be one person" "well if we can manage it right then, yes we would probably see multiple people take the place of mr apple". He paused and looked at his files "do you think we will atual get a convegton". The police man in charge of the case shrugged "with these cases it can be hard to tell". Greg nodded "don't I know

it" "so in the end who knows". Greg
signed and stamped the front of the file
as the case closed.

Chapter

18

______

The final room

If one was to journey to the section of the earth that Mr Apple's main home was located. You would most likely be impressed by the size of the place. The inside of the house, or to be more precise the inside of the mansion was also very incredible. However if a person continued down deep hundreds of feet into the ground one would find many police officers.

The officers groaned as they saw another very long flight of stares. One of them cried out "my god can we please just sit down".however instead of

sitting down they spent more than half
an hour walking down stairs.

* * * *

When the officers reached the first
door of this final level it had taken them
just five minutes of non going down the
stairs to get through. However now that
they were on the tenth door it was
taking them well over an hour to get
through. After a full two weeks of work
they got through the last blockade . Now
they came to another door marked
panic room do not enter as the door is
no longer unlockable once locked.this
door took the officers more than a
month to get through but once they did
they discovered the secrets of the panic
room it became worth it.

* * * *

The desk and chair faced the ten
screens that showed a mix of CCTV
from the house above and of the
bunker. One camera showed the
equipment and other men just outside
the panic room. There was an oxygen
cube to one side with pipes to breathe
from. On one wall was a machine gun
and beside it lay a holster for a revolver.
In a tank next to it were several
piranhas that it was surmised would eat
any food remains. In the tank was a
revolver the piranhas had tried to bite it
but had left it mostly unharmed. Blood
was splattered against the wall and it
appeared as if somebody had been shot.
A tag lay on the ground saying the
words ``the keeper". The blood was
tested and a positive result appeared
for a nineteen year old boy called Kevin
from luxembourg.he had made the
mistake of getting involved in illegal
drugs. This had resulted in him being
given a reduced sentence of five years.
He had left the juvenile detention

centre two years prior after serving
seven years. Three years had been
added for killing a fellow inmate who
was set to give evidence on one of mr
apples distributiors.it was surmised
that Kevin had originally been about to
warn mr apple that the bunker was at
risk of being discovered when he saw
Fred inside the shaft but had not done
so when he saw a body drop the two
floors down. However when he had
seen the advancing police and had tried
to contact Mr Apple however when Mr
Apple's device failed to send the
message and the police found the
trapdoor got some food then locked
down the panic room where he tried to
use the explosives to kill the officers
and trap them. However while the
bunker was airtight the individual
floors had to be closed to make them air
tight the panic room was automatically
airtight. This meant that the explosive
trigger had to be severed from the
explosives. So when that failed he just
waited for the police. Then when the

police came to the panic room floor he
took the gun and shot himself while
standing in the piranhas tank.

Chapter

19

The mortuary

Dave spent his life from the age of three to eighteen going to school and being in school. He then spent his years of eighteen to twenty two going and attending college. When he got out he then spent his time working. All of this meant that Dave had not discovered the rest of the world. So it was with confusion that Dave tried to find the mortuary. Dave had a complex feeling when it came to grace. He had a feeling of something. Not love but of want. And it was for this reason that he had decided to go to the mortary that was in the backend of the city. Dave made his way to the building and knocked on the door. The police man showed him into the room. There was a sheet on the table in the centre and as the mortician took the sheet off Dave could see that there was a body underneath the sheet. Dave saw the naked body of what appeared to be a woman. Dave walked over he felt the need to look down so Dave looked at her body. He said "um i just need to check something". The martian nodded his head in indifference. Dave placed his hands on her breasts "o ya that's the stuff" He squeezed her breasts and touched his lips to her nipples "ya it's her" he said. The police officer looked at him and then winked at the motion "would you like a moment sir" dave looked at him for a second before nodding "yes thank you that would be perfect". The police officer and the other man left the room.

They went down the corridor to go and
watch the mortuaries cctv.

＊＊＊＊

The Morrison was saying "he does know
that we already know she is miss apple
right". The police officer shrugged and
zoomed in on Dave "well he wasn't
taken into confidence".

Chapter 20

Secret pleasure

After the police officer and the mortician left Dave looked around the empty room. The room was mostly bare as Grace's body had not been preserved due to the length of time that she had been dead. The body's that lay on the slabs were covered in cloth. Grace's body had a stench like hot rubbish. But Dave did not care. He came towards the slab that grace's remains lay on, and climed ontop of grace he took all of his cloths off and began to fuck her dead body. He cried out and kissed her broken lips. For the first time Grace's lips were either hot or cold. They were a dull temperature. The lips were cut and bruised. her face before was free from blemishes due to surgery. but now it was bartered and unrecognisable. Dave kept pushing in and out for a full half hour. Her body had rotted slightly and had become stiff but Dave was able to manage.then once he felt he could move on from grace he got off her and pulled his clothes back on he walked out of the notary and thanked the mortician and the police officer. " Thank you for helping me. " The police officer shook his head "no no thank you. " Dave bit his lip and left the room. He stepped out of the building and smiled. It was a new time and he was going to try and enjoy his time.

****

While dave wanted to start afresh The
police officer on the other hand wanted
something else "hey man could you get
me the tapes" .The martian stared at
him "what tapes" then he thought for a
second "on those tapes" "ya i need to
jerk off to something good right" The
martian nodded "ya we have 4k
cameras in there" The police officer
smiled "it'll look real good on my 86
inch tv" "a ha life sized a" "you know it,
Atual i was going to take some of the
other tapes in her room but well they
took it in as evidence before i could get
one" the martian nodded in sympathy
"ya well here you are a nice bit of half
hour entertainment". The police man
nodded and left. The Martian posted the
video online in order to get views for is
pornogorpy account.

* * * * * * *

The car drove into its space and
switched off by the two story house. The

policeman got out of his car and walked up to the door. He took out his key and unlocked the door. He walked down the corridor and put the ready made meal in the microwave. He went to the fridge and took out two beers. The police officer ate his meal and drank a gulp from his beer. The police officer knew full well that his wife was sleeping upstairs but still made more noise than necessary.

One of the children woke up and decided that she would walk down stairs.

Once he was finished his dinner he put his plate in the sink without washing it and walked down the hallway to the living room. The police man sat down on the large couch and took the usb the martian had given him out of his pocket and walked over to the large tv. He plugged the usb in and returned to his couch. He picked up the remote control and pressed the USB button and hit play. The video started and he pulled his

dick out of his pants and groaned as it
began to get hard.

Dave Will Return

In

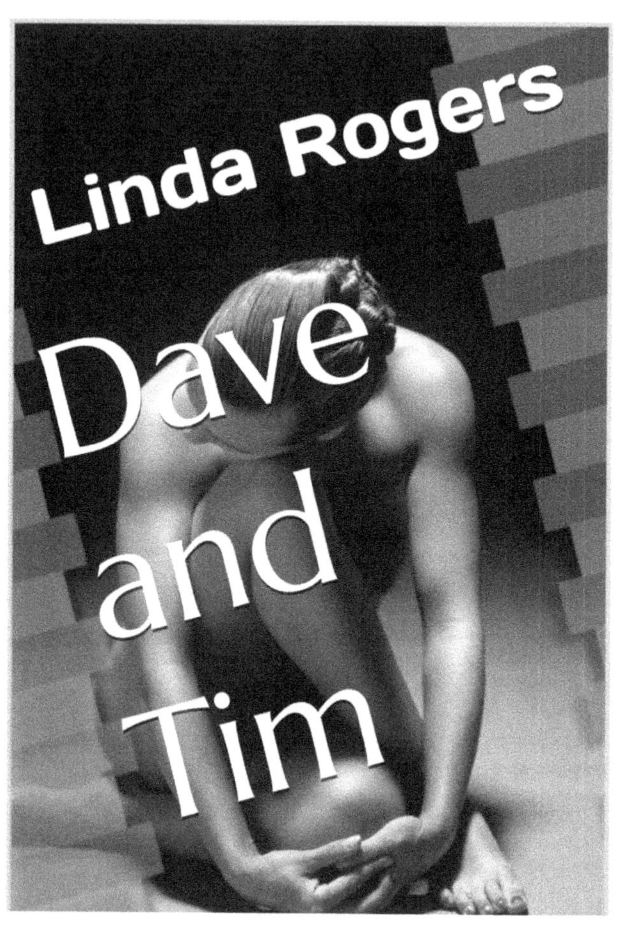

Linda Rogers
Dave
and
Tim

About The Author

Linda Rogers is a young author who tried to write her first published story at 11 years old. Unfortunately they only self published on their website and never sold on an official store. Behind the office doors is the first book published under the linda rogers name on an official store

Thank you for reading

Dave Lives A Normal

everyday life untill one day he is called into his boss's office

* 9 7 9 8 8 4 0 6 9 9 4 8 5 *